Agnomia

Róbert Gál

AGNOMIA

Translated from the Slovak by David Short

DALKEY ARCHIVE PRESS

Originally published in Slovak by Petrus Publishers (Bratislava) as Agnómia in 2008.

First Dalkey Archive edition, 2018.

Library of Congress Cataloging-in-Publication Data
Names: Gál, Róbert, 1968- author. | Short, David, 1943- author.
Title: Agnomia / Róbert Gál ; translated from the Slovak by David Short.
Other titles: Agnomia. English
Description: First Dalkey Archive edition. | McLean, IL : Dalkey Archive Press, 2018.
Identifiers: LCCN 2018026126 | ISBN 9781628972795 (pbk. : acid-free paper)
Classification: LCC PG5439.17.A3 A7413 2018 | DDC 891.8/73--dc23
LC record available at https://lccn.loc.gov/2018026126

Co-funded by the Creative Europe Programme of the European Union

The book has received a subsidy from SLOLIA Committee, the Centre for Information on Literature in Bratislava, Slovakia.

www.dalkeyarchive.com
McLean, IL / Dublin

Printed on permanent/durable acid-free paper

All that is manifest is ruled by desire. —Yes, a son wants to become a father.

František Drtikol

I FIRST MET Eugene K. in New York during the spring of 1993. To this day I can still remember the experience—I can't think what else to call it. It was at a party in the cozy, concrete apartment of Eugene's classmate Leoš R., not far from Columbia University, where both of them were students at the time. I think I was dragged there by C., a girl from my class at the New School. We were like two pairs of tandem riders who went to all kinds of parties with the job of representing our small nations that meant nothing to anybody, on top of which there was an imbalance between us (I mean as Czechs and Slovaks, given that I was the only Slovak). I don't recall exactly what went on at the party, though I do remember that Eugene's boorish humor got on my nerves from the very start and that I was incapable—flustered by the thousand and one other things that were distracting and disturbing me—of concealing my crabbiness and above all my utter indifference to everything that was going on. He came over to me and asked my name, and when C. told him my name was Róbert he couldn't resist launching into something about battery-operated boyfriends, Bobs for short. I don't think even I was able to leave his would-be jocular comment unanswered, and eventually somebody casually asked if my last name happened to be Gál, and that immediately subdued Eugene, who now realized he was standing face to face with the son of an illustrious father. He immediately launched into an almost tearful apology, the asshole, and as is often the case in such situations everyone promptly began confusing me with my father, a *genuine* revolutionary, and taking me for the revolutionary that he had been. But I'm content just to be, as I always tell myself in places where everything militates against it, including my own mind. I can't be bothered to work out the connections between everything and everything else, as people with a general education tend to enjoy doing. Not even when I actually do cast about for such connections do I enjoy it, not even when I comprehend the composition of everything and everything else as indicative of the certainty of the existence of a particular item within the whole, the realness of which, having trekked throughout the sphere of my mind, is capable of reconstituting the bulk of the items of that whole, like filling the gaps in a collection. Randomly unknocked-out teeth, it occurs to me in due course, as I link one thing to another (with obligatory integration to a third thing). We're in New York, my pillion rider tells me with a slight smile, as she and I wander to the inner pulsation of that city's streets, and, investing the unspoken with the force of each moment that will never be repeated, she repeats the same sentence to me over and over again. For the author wants to tell his tale, but doesn't know where to begin, and he doesn't even know if there is a tale to be told at all. He tries to get inside it, as if any entrance on his part would automatically coordinate with the context in which the tale is being played out. Coordinate with what is being played out, whatever that might be, on a parasitical basis, though it's erroneously taken to be symbiotic. And so our author is back in the present. He has just bought a practical set of portable loudspeakers. And now he's trying to work out (prematurely perhaps?) what he actually needs them for. A lawn party with a computer, or a bench party with an iPod? He wonders. In the former case a small audience would certainly make sense. And in the latter? Would it not be better to play the music into himself, through earphones? This question takes him back to New York and stirs up a number of memories of his time as a student and of all that went with it. For example, the period spent in the typical West Village apartment belonging to an aging and divorced model with a prodigious memory, lovingly duplicated in the mass of objects that it would be a sin to throw out. In the realm of tucked-away memories he, too, might be satisfied with that little windowless room, with its gloriously antique foldaway table "from Europe," on top of which he'd kept the antediluvian computer that had to be fed with physical startup disks every time it was switched on, and he'd been in absolute raptures over it. At the time he was working on a study in which he sought to connect Heidegger with an authentic experience he'd had in the city, which he construed, in a manner uniquely his own, as the reified model of a sacred space. Sometimes he would take a stroll along these wild streets, awash with junkies and illusions, taking the landlady's impeccably well-behaved dog for a walk, at which times he felt like a genuine spoiled young *New Yorker of good family*. And seeking reasons for a Yes where a pre-defined No might explode spontaneously; by repeated attempts at suicide and the like. Because in every Yes that is forced by a No the image of each is bisected equally *in the latter.* In the evenings he would bang away on the synthesizer he'd bought with his grant money, and through the earphones of his portable CD player he'd listen to the complete works of Stravinsky, Schoenberg, and Beethoven, a totally new world to him, and during that time he would have a powerful sense of spiritual dilatation. That apart, he ate hotdogs—so as to save up for the music—and in the evenings he used to go to his favorite Bagel Buffet, open 24/7, which was the only place in the city where he could focus properly on the Nietzsche he was in the middle of reading. Instability as a defense against manipulation? "It may be said," someone has recently written of Kafka, "that never in the course of his entire life was he a whole man, he was never in the right place, he was never genuine, not even to himself. But on the other hand he was able thereby to resist pressures from without and never to become what others wanted him to be." I've just been reading a newspaper interview with the icon of Slovak pop culture when I was young, Jožo Ráž, the lead singer of the band Elán. He says that the top dogs of the erstwhile communist regime were actually "kind old souls" who wouldn't harm a fly. L. and I are sitting in a genteel coffee shop where I'm telling her she absolutely must read the interview. A few days later she sends me a text message, thanking me for the tip; she's read the interview and found it, as she puts it, "interesting." She goes on to say that she's in no mood to argue with Ráž's novel ideas on the subject of communism vis-à-vis capitalism—chiefly on the ways in which, vis-à-vis capitalism, communism is better—but on other subjects she says she appreciates the plain speaking of somebody she knows as a farrago of foolhardiness, naiveté, and arrogance. "SEXISM IS FASCISM," someone has sprayed in black on the red door of a sex shop in Kreuzberg, Berlin. I've bought a secondhand Peugeot bicycle. It looks good and it's lightweight and handles like a dream. The guy who sold it to me compares its cream color to the color of champagne. "What do you do?" asks a classmate of yore when we bump into each other fifteen years later in Brno. "I write," I reply with well-concealed embarrassment. An hour later, somebody else asks me the same question. I reply: "I'm looking for a story." I'm in the reopened Štefánka coffee house in the very heart of Bratislava, having a drink and a chat with a young poet and organizer of literary festivals, who tells me enthusiastically about the other poets who used to sit over a drink in this same place many years ago. Ján Smrek, for instance. On the Internet, I open one of Smrek's collections. And in a poem about the beautiful nightclub dancer Ellén, I read: *Oh, so dark your eyes, / those almonds full of feeling, / they're the eyes of a child! / How misspent on earthly passions wild, / how misspent that the Jew / should make them subject of his dealings!* Hm! Thank you very much, Mr. Smrek. So "Jew" equals "sexist," does it? *Remember me to the mother who, / while still her daughter Mary, / for a bag of gold did place you / in that tycoon's hands so hairy.* We'll come back to the hairs. Does anything else need to be said on the quality of this jingle? Childish dealings, feelings wildish. . . And I ask: What are the limits to what one can make resolutions about? Is it possible to resolve upon, say, a zest for life? Despite all the anti-amenities of a racial or hairy kind? The next thing is that you'll be blaming a girl for being a girl, a mother for being a mother, and a guy who enters a nightclub to watch the striptease for being a pervert! Don't you find that slightly muddled? But let's move on to another neck of the woods, so we don't end up putting down too many roots here. ("Because you were the nerve of your family!" as my shrink once told me.) Protracted, unfulfilled expectations leave their trace on one, but that doesn't require one to identify with all the woes of the world. All the woes of the world as an abstraction extracting long-unfulfilled expectations, which thereby end up being even more protracted and even more unfulfilled. One idea and its successors. Can a woman be an idea? Something that is predefined, such as a generation, that is subsequently only gradually filled up with people and ideas. The constant steering of how things evolve in the form of parental admonitions. If this, then that: look and you'll see! The artificially fabricated causality of what has been commanded, which has to be constantly prodded along, or so it seems. Nothing tangible, and yet it has to be constantly prodded toward some point just to prove that one is right about it. The question is: On what basis can we measure the justifiability of that prodding, and is prodding even the issue? Because whatever the eternity, one's power over time is equally unlimited. Revealing a pain gripped by the anxiety coiled around it. The gyrations of matter wondrously endowed with energy, of whatsoever that energy might be. Permanent Yes and No, killing each other in an exuberant typhoon of suicides. Because we won't find a thing just through seeking out a word by which to name it. Though on the other hand, a degree of heuristic enthusiasm might be no bad thing. For is there any point in talking about the past other than looking for links between one enthusiasm and another from one time to another? We're in New York, says C., my pillion rider, as if the sentence were an incantation. We're in New York, she repeats, and the words reflect states of different worlds like cannabine wafts of neat tomorrows from dug-up todays. We need but to pinch ourselves to believe. She's looking at me with that serpentine gaze of a young Prague intellectual who has come to New York at her parents' expense to seek analogies between this and that and to talk twaddle. There's a pile of books on the desk from which she would be forever copying out bits and pieces. Once she took me to a pseudo-intellectual hellhole to meet some feminists. The whole ambience had me feeling quite sick. Scuttling about among all those women with their outsize egos, and attending to their needs, was the only man (most likely a homosexual), he being the life partner of the chief feminist, a plump intellectual who was positively scary. Coming back once from a late-night bar, we saw a dark-skinned couple hollering at each other across the width of the street and it all sounded quite dramatic. C. says that sadomasochistic relationships between black people are quite common. And another time she locked me in a classroom to show me all the scars on her tongue and ask me all sorts of inane questions. But otherwise we got along well together. "I want *you*," I tell her without meaning it in the slightest. Her sweaty friend with the bald head is sitting a short way off enthusiastically spinning some yarn. The company bursts out laughing. My angst only deepens. I gaze into her dark, watery eyes, which seem intent on devouring me on the spot, but then they balk. Her face immediately puts on a mask, and even before anything issues forth from her delicately fashioned mouth, she adopts an expression of indifference, followed at once by the glaring cold of disdain. And yet, something did flash across her face. For only a fraction of a second, barely detectable, and yet that telltale, momentary slackening of her defense mechanisms was there. "I'm a *femfatal*," she was shouting, and the way she moved was like skittish mercury bouncing around. First she went for a pee, then we darted into the rear section of the auditorium, in the dark most of the seats were vacant. There was a slight creak. I placed one hand on her half-naked thigh and with a gyrating motion we jointly converged on her private parts. Peter Brötzmann, saxophone in hand, and another musician with a trumpet were disgorging into the air a sophisticated jumble of sounds, looking like windblown plants bending now this way, now that. The glorious wailing of their instruments was colorfully backed by the evocative pulsing of bass and percussion. In a moment of magnetic petrification, I watched her face and empathized as, to the fitful rhythm of the music, which might have been chaotic but certainly not without order, she reached her first orgasm. Like a child learning to walk: at first it hops around a bit. At one of Mike Patton's '90s concerts with Faith No More in Chile some pot-valiant members of the audience started spitting at the band on stage. Patton responded by goading the spitters on, and they weren't just supposed to go on, but to go further, and he offered them his own wide-open mouth, with which he then carried on singing. But musicians have an easier time of it than wordsmiths—that's struck me so many times before. Because they lack—and don't even need—that firm focus on each and every unit of a word whose creator rises up like one reborn because of it. A musician doesn't need to keep rising up again, he's here already and anything he creates is more or less incidental. Reproducing the state of the moment and reproducing the state of the world are two different things. The future already there in the past, if incognito? Everyone has told me everything and no one even opened his mouth. That horrifies me sometimes. Each and every person's infinite self-conceit from each and every person's own position. Nothing that is finite about that position can have any claim to *its own* infinity. *We* are infinity and for us the finite—and anything finite can be torn asunder—always makes good fodder. For how is it possible to look for something that's coming when something is always coming? Time is money. Yes? Or: Time is regard for, observance of the affairs of another. The regard, or observance, of the observant, not of an observer fascinated by how an object of his observation balks at being observed. You go to a concert and well-bred musicians will thank you for coming. Not with that all-embracing, applause-anticipating bow, but with an ordinary *Thank you* addressed almost personally to each and every person present. I saw this for myself at an experimental music club, The Stone, in New York. Now that was *some* concert! In Slovakia it's different. In Slovakia, naturally creative people are unnaturally hemmed in by rules, as if their need and desire to discover something had to be a kind of given, present in them to their dying day and serving to distinguish them from all ordinary mortals. Not that ordinary mortals are in danger of this; it's more a trap that will sooner or later ensnare the ones whose lot it is to stand out against any such narrow-mindedness. Strong wine before bed and strong coffee after rising. I'm once again reminded of Nietzsche, a philosopher who, just so that he *could* get to sleep, *had to* dose himself up for the night, and in the morning he *was not to* forget to measure out the right daytime dose of his medicine so that he could get up. And his spirit, which leaves the body as cigarette smoke leaves a cigarette. And then his sober psyche can take a photograph of himself. And he *is*. Memories are forms of possibility in the past. Memories and dreams are one and the same. Sunk in my own thoughts after a pleasant evening stroll, I'm returning home to polish off an open bottle and plunge into sleep. I let some music in through my earphones at the very moment that I get ready to enjoy a swig of good wine. Then comes a track by Boredoms, the Japanese rock band, one I'd never heard before. Throughout the entire song, the band's frontman, Yamantaka Eye, emitted a stream of sounds reminiscent of vomiting by means of a convincing croaking in his *throat*. I had to switch the music off briefly so as not to be put off my wine. And that compelled me to muse briefly on the philosophical nature of the question of how art might convey a real sense of reality in such a way that the reality conveyed might appear real and also that the art of conveying it might be considered conveyed art. Entering the undefined on a graph using the principle of psychophysical parallelism. Cutting off the body in such a way that a bubble of the spirit commensurate to it... I'm gazing at a tree-shrub hastily planted in a demolished square. I want to tie the moon in with it so that the image I'm creating looks fully formed. It's a full moon. Is it fulfilled? My room is inhuman. It isn't accessed by a door, but by clockwork, with a key poking from outside in. A bit like a deep intake of breath whose exhalation and exhaustion are identical. Music has an instant effect. That's something it shares with a drug or a telling aphorism. Circular self-relocation, each time a total gyration round one of a pair of aching legs. Oneness with pain like a fly with a wing torn off. The whirling of a whirligig beetle. Extirpation of redundancy by stretching it on the rack of a thing that at that instant is no longer a problem. "Don't call it a problem," my father says. (It isn't a problem, says Magritte's pipe. The umbrella and sewing machine giggle.) Striding smoothly off into oneself as if it were a kind of exit. A blow to the head is followed by a muted obscuration, one circle petering out in another. An odd thing: Five years ago, I promised my dentist—she'd asked what I did for a living—that I would write five books. That's to say, I told her that it was normal for me to write one book a year, and I haven't been to see her in five years. That's called trial by time. Circular motion. A certain critic said of Thomas Bernhard that few authors had succeeded in extracting so much that's positive from their obsessions. Snow White is the aggregate of the Seven Dwarfs. Time was when I derived a strange satisfaction from comparing photos of myself with a Hungarian sportsman who was my namesake. He, always on a track specially tailored to him and others like him, and I, affecting the Decadent poet in a favorite all-night clubroom. I can call to mind various events in my life that have invariably called this dichotomy to mind ad hoc. For instance, the colossal frame of my friend Jaro D., who, if he wanted, could dispatch anyone with a single blow. Yet, despite that, he was of an ultra-sentimental disposition; I can't recall him doing even a scintilla of harm to a single soul. It was more as if anything that Jaro D. ever considered significant needed its significance to be enhanced by someone else's remarking on its significance to him. With the obvious exception of certain prima facie eccentricities that my impulsive temperament sometimes just couldn't resist, such as jointly tossing empty bottles out of student dorm windows onto harmlessly parked cars and suchlike. On the other hand, he found nothing abnormal about copying other people's pictures and publishing them in mimeographed magazines under his own name. "Sorry about that time when I couldn't resist the urge that upended you into a slowly gathering pool of blood," I apologize years after the event to a classmate I happen to run into at someone's birthday party. He takes the story further than the one bit I remember. He says the situation had turned to my disadvantage. I, the punch-thrower, flat on my back, and the blood, streaming out of his mouth into my face, visibly tainting me. A postscript arrives in his evening email: "It's interesting that you've banished from your mind any recollection of my attack on you. Meanwhile, I have no recollection of your action that provoked my bloody reaction." And all truths come together in a Gordian knot of falsehood. (For falsehood is one and truths are many.) Can solitude be universal? In what sense? In the sense of the shot-out windows of abandoned houses, in which there's no room even for dogs? So where's that distant barking coming from? And what is it seeking to say? Is lamentation a form of discourse? By virtue of what? I return in my memory to the many times L. and I had sat together. I recall her flitting through space, her hopelessly callous pretense at being motionless that required anyone else to get every watchword wrong. As if each sentence uttered necessarily required a correction in the sentence that followed. She fastens on your lips as on a flower she's pollinating. She pulls you into her eyes and with each word spoken she imprints her verdict on your trembling heart. And you repay her with counter-attacks, constantly attenuating that chimerical being to the level of the image that her insatiability tirelessly sustains within you. I had a dream: "By then Kant may have been legitimate, but he only really registered with the public after he began urinating on stage," it said in the snippet from a barely legible copy of a piece in the daily *Sme* that another of the guests at this remarkable hotel had brought me, with the words, "You left this behind"—so much for dreams. The article was one of the more substantial reviews of my recently published book of aphorisms. The review had reached me sort of late in the day, after I'd had a run-in with my father. I don't remember exactly who passed it on to me, but most likely it was my mother with the off-the-cuff remark: "Look, they're singing your praises." I also recall the picture set opposite the review and captured then and there by my photographic memory, a photo of the kind described as "for illustration purposes only" and filling an entire page, depicting a kind of geyser-like spouting on canvas, downswept, upswept, and on and on, like paint sprayed indiscriminately with a sputtering brush that has lent immediate expression to the whole by smearing the streaks across the canvas. It reminded me of the series of *self-naked* portrayals of L.'s body that I'd used in another book of aphorisms, when I'd enabled the lady photographer to create an intimate document of our cohabitation. The public knows the outcome. On the basis of the photos, the book's publisher and a number of the publisher's steadfast reviewers made the author out to be a pervert. Yet the reality was quite different. It was a joke similar to Kant's deliberate pissing on stage to win the notice of the public. But even onstage peeing has its rights and wrongs, which Kant had failed to appreciate fully at the time, just like the author of a book of philosophy containing pictures of a naked girl, who was described by some critic as androgynous. The thing is, by the act of self-portraiting, the girl was "pissing on herself," as we

Slovaks say—meaning that she didn't give a damn about herself or what she was doing, but in the process of the shoot, she underwent a fatefully positive transformation, as did the author, who, however, frankly confesses to the fact of his own spiritual transformation in the book's afterword. And now another interpretation of the whole thing occurs to him in the form of the statements: "Kant pissed on the audience. / Cunt pissed on the audience." The audience could piss off for all the pisser cared, perhaps. I'm in a late-night laundromat on Bergmannstrasse in Berlin. It's nearing eleven o'clock. With undisguised fascination I watch the drums of the washing machines as they turn commensurately with the gradual purging of their contents, leading to their final cleansing. Through my earphones, Ennio Morricone intrudes on the scene as he plays the yet-unlearned stories of my life. A talented poet, a girl with the face of a doll, confides to me by email that Berlin is her unfulfilled dream. Can I empathize with her case enough that my sense of guilt at having spilled someone's dream into the dream of someone else will actually become agonizing? But where's there any fulfilling of dreams while the washing machine is still going? To reach the brink of genius and stop just before it, trailing behind me the entirety of a squandered life. That is one option. And another is simply to jump across the brink. I'm looking at that memorable photo from 1976 in which the charismatic octogenarian Léon Theremin is presenting his invention, later named after him—that remarkable musical instrument that emits sounds from the cosmic spheres—standing at his right hand under his watchful gaze, his nine-year-old grandniece, Lydia Kavina, the last pupil he taught to play the instrument, who is gazing through the fingers of her right hand, in a gesture of quaint enlightenment. Her left hand is being held gently, yet firmly, at the correct height by the maestro himself, who has a rather fatherly air about him. The little girl's hair, neatly woven into two plaits, is adorned with a huge white ribbon. Visible at the front is her neatly knotted Young Pioneer scarf, which is in sharp contrast (the photo is black-and-white) to the white, starched blouse beneath it. As if it were some kind of colloquium, with the audience in tense expectation of the end of the story, so that at its conclusion they might spontaneously demonstrate their admiration with applause for both the scientist and his talented young charge, the little virtuosa. The instrument looks like a wooden birdhouse, with a kind of two-pronged metal handle poking out of one side and an antenna on the other side—and between the two is where the tension arises that is used to produce the sounds. The unique feature of the invention is that it can, indeed must, be played without actually being touched. It's a musical instrument that can evoke the ungraspable directly and literally. I summon up from my memory another photo from eight or nine years ago. It looks as if it had been scrawled on glossy paper using the make-the-best-of-it method and shows the following: me sitting on a wooden chair at a round table in our regular coffee place, jotting down something or other and wearing an expression of self-importance. With my delicate fingers I'm signing a book or noting down some idea I've had. My long, shaggy hair is falling naturally across my shoulders. She is sitting just below me in the photo and, watching me from that position, she looks as if she's breathing me in. Her expression is benign, tender, solicitously devout. As if she were longing, once and for all, to embrace my entire being and never let me out of her arms. Now I'm looking at another of the photos you took. Decadent as the sun, you're looking at me here and now, eyes staring into the mirror of back then. And you dragged me down, come on, and I posed for you. The concept of a photo composed in halves, one half showing me absorbed in thought, and the other with you focused on me. The unforced force of rejection portrayed as a negative, hence as if forced, with direct oversight of the downfall, whose allure is in the spot-lit contours of the faces. When the sun becomes a hostage, pain is surgically removed. Three young female artists are presenting their projects. One of them, a well-known photographer of the rediscovered theme of female bodies, has come up with a project consisting of a collection of cardboard boxes into each of which some idea has been ingeniously glued, like the jack-in-the-box contrivance in a cuckoo clock. I'm sitting with the woman at a table in the timeless space of a café, letting her spill over me waves of her accumulated anxiety that stems from the fact that one of her colleagues is almost her complete look-alike. She describes her step by step, in utter distress. "Young, beautiful, passionate. And relentless in pursuit of her objectives." "Just like you," I say. "Yes, you're right," she replies with a slight sigh. I relocate to the shabby old building of a former railway station. I enter its scruffy bar. Leading directly from the door there are a few steps that have to be descended in a ritual, theatrical manner, each new arrival on the scene being subject to thorough and silent scrutiny by pairs of watchful eyes. The tension between the regulars and me is almost unbearable, and yet I walk on, heading straight for the bar. I order a beer and settle down at a little table just beyond the bar, strategically protected by the counter from any possible attacks by the invisible regulars. They, however, slowly become visible. They are people with the brooding, ponderous features and deep-set eyes of old men. The first one my gaze settles on could easily have been Samuel Beckett in his old age. Taciturn and photogenic, with an elegant peaked cap on his head like a union boss. I can see the other guests as well, each like a living monument, sitting at his own hulking wooden table, and all with exactly the same cap on their heads. One of them has in front of him an open newspaper in which he's engrossed. I've turned up right in the middle of an argument: the regulars are trying to persuade the bartender of the necessity of some measure or other, but the man behind the bar is wearing a bulletproof expression. Instead of replying to a direct question from one of his patrons, who is pointing a finger at him as the only proper addressee for the question raised, the bartender suddenly picks up a newspaper from a nearby table, opens it, and hides his entire face behind it. This particular day the newsprint is as black as soot. There must be a reason for that too. The first Russian president, Boris Yeltsin, is dead, I read. And then I dreamed that I was passing through the reception area of a student dorm, posing as a woman. One of the girls was leaving to visit her parents and so she had the staff assign me to her bed. In the morning, I cheerfully rose and introduced myself to the two guys casually chatting away on the adjacent beds—this time giving my real name. Then I asked them whether I could stay there for a week, since this was what the girl and I had agreed on. "Sure," they said. We're outside on some grass and the birds of the air are all atwitter. I say to the boys: "Look, I've got a real blockbuster here! Perhaps we could do it as a performance." And from my bag I take the precious contraband in the form of a musical composition: *Six Litanies for Heliogabalus*. I put it on. The music starts up ritualistically, full-on from the very outset. Just at the point where the regular pounding of the drums comes in (constantly fired up by the guttural shrieking of the singer), people were already happily dancing on the meadow. A surrealist painter, watching it from the requisite safe distance, writes in his diary: "The fucking trash's been at it since first thing." A smaller group of dancers like a wriggling caterpillar is moving off up the hill. Then it's the turn of the real, unadulterated "voodoo section" of the piece. And now a kind of totem is coming. "They're not going to chop somebody in four, are they?" somebody in the assembled crowd can be heard saying. Coming with objectivity, waves in which objectivity comes. Objectivity is never objective. In an aside about one of Hegel's books, Kierkegaard declared that if the author had noted in the preface that his book was no more than an intellectual experiment, it would have been a remarkable work. But Hegel made no such note, which is why his ideas are ludicrous. This reminds me of one almost expunged snippet from my relationship with L. On one occasion, as I was leaving to go somewhere, I took a condom out of my bag in her presence, meaning to transfer it to a secret pocket in my anorak. And she immediately started remonstrating with me, failing to see why I needed a condom in a secret pocket since I had her. I didn't know what to say. Perhaps that the condom was a kind of good-luck charm, sustaining my hope for better things to come? During his time as a student in New York, the author of these notes was still, if memory serves, a virgin. He opens his diary with the comment that seeks to capture this fact in a relevant manner. It states: "Long maintained virginity is doubtless somehow linked to a future openness toward the young." And it adds that the remark was made alongside a reference to Kundera's *Immortality*, noting that the great Goethe had only lost his virginity at the ripe old age of forty. Yesterday, I met Ben for the first time in two years at a literary evening. I asked him whether he was back in Prague now or whether he was only visiting and meant to return to Japan. He said living in Japan was impossible. Two years previously he'd said the same thing about Prague. "Tell me something about Berlin," he says. "My wife's just applied to go to college there." To this day I don't know his wife's name, because any time Ben talks about his wife, he uses the expression "my wife." As I interpret it, this implies a kind of balance between the two words, which are of equal importance. One pointing to the fact of *ownership*, and the other pointing to the *object* of that ownership, in other words, the socially defined entity that is a wife. He spoke of her psychological anomaly, which he'd discovered only of late, after their relationship had already lasted many years. I told him that when I first met his wife, she struck me as. . . hypersensitive. I called it that for want of any better word, and maybe out of a degree of tact. The evening continued with a reading (in English) that flooded the whole interior of the moderately humanized, industrially metallic organism that was the pub. I asked a friend, the Slovak sitting next to me, whether he was getting anything out of it. He replied that he was getting nothing, though he was plainly enjoying himself. He said that it reminded him of the sermons at Sunday mass, where his grandmother used to take him at the age of six or seven. The rest of the evening was epitomized by the bewitching Markéta, who, after a dose of marijuana combined with plum brandy, was in such a peculiar state of mind that she needed to bring to life the body language of some sun-worshipping goddess of antiquity. Her hands were like the pans of scales, and her gaze, discharging rays in incandescent chains that bombarded the darkened interior of the place with their crystallized magnetism, was what the scale pans were weighing. In retrospect, this now strikes me as having been a kind of unavoidable, ongoing tug-of-war between gazes, during which I couldn't help feeling entirely capable of devouring what she was emitting as an unusual, yet legitimate, kind of nourishment. And that filled me with an absolute sense of victory. In the final stage of this game, Markéta, by now staring at the quartered emblem of a compound cunt (from a photo taken by the Slovak photographer Miro Š. and printed on the front of my black T-shirt in a garish green), spews into the ether a curse that had something to do with a spider. She can't work out what the thing on my T-shirt is a photo of, and I can't tell her, because by doing so I would break through the ice that holds things together, and the truth as uttered by me would instantly start to smack of overstatement. Because, for any reality to be generalized, it inevitably lacks something. "What's the matter, my little one?" L. asks, now two heads taller than me again. As a child, I often tried to imagine what a doll would do if it suddenly came to life. But what does it mean to be someone's doll from the perspective of divine providence? Isn't our God just an enfant terrible who can't play properly and watches from on high to see what his toys down here are up to? Let us take evil as an alternative version of good, good with evil *deputizing* for it. As the evil of *opting* for evil when the good to which we pertain is felt by us as evil. For one does have a need to say something, but words get in the way. Words have no need to say anything. That's the problem. The problem of the whole of literature. And then there are expressions that we instantly snare by memory, having an immediate appreciation of how crucial they are. Memes? In the Czech environment one such example in recent years would be "to have fun." There's this American director of experimental films and he and I have been considering the possibility of doing something together, a kind of set of tableaux vivants to go with John Zorn's *Six Litanies*. In terms of its theme, I see it as a blunt critique of the hedonism in which our civilization has become so deeply mired. (Is hedonism a form of rebellion? For example, Artaud saw Heliogabalus as a rebel, not a madman. Where is the limit beyond which all hedonism is vacuous?) How odd: in the utterance of grand words, I find I'm up against a degree of self-denial. It's as if the sound of a word is in contrast to its meaning, as if certain sounds were unworthy of the importance of their meanings, and vice versa. I'm most aware of this with such Italian words as *cappuccino* or *stracciatella*. . . It's the other way round with words like *autonomy* or *identity*. In the former case one seems driven to go after a word's sound, in the latter its meaning. In either instance there's this disturbing sense of becoming the word's hostage. I can't forget little N., with her head held high, yet oddly forward-leaning on her slender, tense neck, as if it were holding on there by force, as if it were longing to break free so that it might be exhibited instead as a message constructed from the litmus of its own morality, as the head of a Medusa whose remote functionality only comes into play once it has been ripped off and is in the hands of someone else. The consistent automatic head-nodding, the puppet-play fast-motion "Yes" of hers. The consistent sharp-focus look in her eyes that only ever see what they themselves radiate because the glare gives them an existential certitude. Anyone who is confident at the moment of saying "Yes" cannot be thinking. It is merely an extended extremity of the urge to have order in things, and that is all one needs. But objects don't need to have order in things, because order is not an attribute of objects. Order is not a matter of objects, but of objectivity, tending toward precision. This could be sensed from her summary gesture, of whose uncompromising urgency she was in all likelihood unaware. All the indications are that she apprehended precision vis-à-vis objectivity—and the full gravity of this burden—as something that applied *a priori* and so wasn't up for discussion. Like a nanny goat peeing on corrugated iron: a loose definition of her stroboscopic laughter. "What came out of my mouth at his death was actually a jibe," she repeats, as if the reasons behind a death have been planned. And could the reasons behind even a suicide case have caused any major upset to the plan? Then there are those suicide procrastinators, past masters at the art of suffering, whose faces are mimetically mute for years on end. And truths mucked out from the depths of their defenselessness as falsehoods. For at each moment in the course of a thought, having a sense of objectivity is actually subjective, though thoughts come about in no other way. A thought doesn't think about what it's thinking about while it isn't a thought yet—a thought doesn't think at all. In embryo, a thought is invariably, inevitably impulsive, and as it is gradually disseminated it starts to flag. The barbed tactility of fingers. "You're hurting me invisibly," she says. As if the pain she feels had been my intention? On top of that, there's her extraordinarily highly developed sensitivity to falls and fractures. ("Caution, risk of electric shock"—as applied not to high-voltage cables but to drunks who've fallen to the ground—has never meant a thing to her.) My defenses against how she feels about things could therefore not fail to be roused, even if there was no sadism in it. Georges Bataille may speak of laughter in deadly earnest, that's to say, without humor, though my own preference is for humor, even at the expense of laughter. "It strikes me as undignified," Jan says, "to accept congratulations for the past, as if that part of it that is not liable to chronological foreshortening were entirely irrelevant. That's not to castigate heroism but to castigate the need to make heroism an object of admiration, as if any act of heroism were admirable, and the rest not. Is this not about the conventional confusion between socially defined heroism and an act of heroism that is supremely individual, and therefore socially indefinable? Where is the boundary between the necessity of a heroic act by a socially defined hero and the necessity of a heroic act by a hero defined *eo ipso* as the actant of a heroic act who has no need for the fact to be proclaimed socially?" Jan asks. Jan is the hero of an invisible reign of terror. Whenever revolt is brewing, it is punished. And since any revolt has already been punished while still only brewing, the ferment can never come to fruition except as impaired. This is true of all Jan's relationships, which never have happy endings. We're talking about the obverse of something one-sided, which is by definition invisible, because it's in the shadow of our hero. What is played out in a shadow can only be seen from within the shadow, and then only if the shadow begins to speak. And then we have to differentiate between what the shadow is saying and the fact that it's being said by a shadow. A man who is deprived of amazement is immediately amazed at what he is being deprived of. And one deprived of amazement doesn't himself know what he is being deprived of. But even he knows that what he is being deprived of is neither random nor a trifle. "Personality surely doesn't stand on the soft horizon of a sob," says my father with a conviction that he brings me round to by not admitting any of my objections. And this forces me to start up my systems of defense mechanisms, so that the accumulation of my *screams directed inward* gradually prevent my exterior from having a face of its own that might point to the nature of my interior. This is how the need arises to compare one's inner state with the exterior aspect of this or that milieu.

Probing commandments propounding errors that from the standpoint of truth command truths. Evidence of conviction confirmed by dogged reaffirmation? And then there are all those unexplored areas of the badly posed question. Standardized obsessions that fit the scheme of some "ism," or open obsessions guzzling breath in fits of clairvoyance. And in the stirring up of tension between the two types of obsession a third type comes into being, one that does find order in its quest for the order within chaos that is shattered by thoughts directed toward a final unraveling along a single trajectory. To show one's true colors means to enhance the tonality of contrast, bestowing sweaty T-shirts on the backs of the generations that will tacitly brand us as the parties guilty of our own misdemeanors. A circle is always one-sided, which is inevitably contingent on the direction in which it is spinning. In practice, speeding up its revolutions means that any vision of its end naturally blurs into a vision of its beginning. Launching oneself off from any point on a circle is admittedly possible, though it cannot be entirely at random.

Grasping the regular patterns of these banalities will help us move on any which way we like! For only a cynic can claim that which side of the bed we get out of doesn't matter in the slightest. Swallowing the sourness of a smile with an awareness of both sourness and smile. And so on. Transforming form through content is not just playing with language. It is about the necessity of preserving form and thereby displaying the content. As in music, here, too, it's not about ideas, it's about the permanent tension arising from the need to think, it's about being appurtenant to a content up to the point of accepting it the way a parasite does. And since the scalpel of one's intellect is not always capable of distinguishing between an operation and an autopsy, the object to be incised is initially abstract, emerging only during the act itself from the mists of ignorance into the sphere of cognition, gradually to acquire the features of a reality of which one is truly aware. A reality whose existence is devitalized by autopsy, but is not actually dead, because it still *is*. When Blevin showed up in Jerusalem with a massive suitcase, I happened to be there. I can recall the burning flare in his eyes, which engaged me at once because it was strikingly at odds with a fragility in his personality, as perhaps also with the fact that he was so short in stature when compared to the dimensions of his luggage. Felix and I are sitting in a small pizzeria, waiting for him, and as soon as he shows up we order some pizza for all three of us. Felix is delighted to be seeing his friend after so many years and at once starts excitedly explaining something to do with the fact that they don't actually have anywhere to stay, but that "It doesn't matter, the main thing is that you're here." I have a pretty clear recollection of my second meeting with Blevin as well. It was in a small house in the rural hinterland of Jerusalem, a part called Ein Karem; I arrived there, at Felix's invitation, shortly after noon one day in spring, and after hammering on the wooden door for a while (following a silent dialogue with the neighbor's dog, chained to its kennel), I was eventually invited in by a half-asleep Blevin, who didn't even seem to recognize me. His heavy-lidded eyes didn't suggest the bleariness of sleep, but were due, as I was soon told, to the long hours of meditation in his ideally suited garret. On a spacious, and yet somehow ineptly constructed wooden desk near one wall, Blevin had plastered the drawers with dozens of stickers bearing sundry maxims, injunctions, and bits of life advice. They were spaced out in a regular pattern dictated by some *neurotic sense of order* and were meant to keep Blevin constantly in mind of the strict, once-and-for-all differences between the desirable and the undesirable, of the way some authority before him had engraved them into words and so immortalized them in these particular forms. And in a monastery park in the middle of Prague, a family of peacocks is strolling about unconstrained. The majesty of the widely admired father peacock is suddenly disturbed when one of the visitors to the park opens a bag of birdseed, just like a previous occasion, when an old lady, who first frightened the bird, then ostentatiously fed him her crumbs, finally, as if that wasn't enough, squawked in surprise: "Ugh, he's gone an' crapped on me!" But let's get back to Jan. Jan is a terrorist without a cause. He's a hundred times brighter than most mortals, but he still lacks what it would take to make him truly wise. He's like a lion with caged eyes, beaming his gaze into eyes that are equally caged. This system of cages is a complex product of his own caged brain. It's a language he opens with every word, only to encase it all over again in one and the same thought. For years, Jan had honed his girlfriend, "to give her added value," but eventually she wanted to have a baby, so she married a tractor driver. Yes, anybody who sees Czechs or Slovaks anywhere abroad tends to wonder: What did these people come here to represent? And then a second question immediately springs to mind: Can, say, a Slovak, as a Slovak, feel democratic anywhere other than in Slovakia? And this leads consequentially to other questions, which, once one has mentally posed them and immediately answered them, lead to a gradual appreciation of why most citizens of small, insignificant countries remain stuck in them as if there were no other option. It is precisely in small and insignificant countries that we encounter writers who take it for granted that they are reproducers of reality, but *why* reality needs to be reproduced they don't reveal. Claiming—as we do—that reality shouldn't be artistically *reproduced* but *produced*, we also should probably separate "work of art" from "art." Some controversial Jewish dude named Eli Roth can turn up and run around shooting his chainsaw massacre in tiny Slovakia, and the Slovaks' first response is outrage, but then they realize they've got a great bit of PR that could bring Slovakia to wider notice. Just one of these *young Tarantinos*, and in no time at all he's achieved something far beyond the efforts of several dozen members of the intellectual elite. True, people can sense what other people are feeling and then treat them accordingly. And in the process, they can also be quite nasty. And those whose lot it's been to be tossed around in the waters of their own turmoil have always been at a disadvantage. Jan introduced me, one by one, to all of his female hostages. He drew me into his underhanded chat-up maneuvers, the outcome of which was ever more distraught looks from the one of the six between whom and himself he would place me as part-actant and part-observer, thereby indirectly replicating my own private hang-up—that is, the Oedipus complex, or the unattainability of one person through another. In this sense, Jan functioned as my psychologist, though more subconsciously than consciously, because sadists don't think that way. Jan always seizes on one of his six, the rest rotate according to a fixed schedule. One is, accordingly, always manifest, with five latent. They're all so devoted to him that none of them would dare have a boyfriend. Jan would only find out anyway, they tell themselves, and spend their evenings masturbating, thinking of Jan. Why do we persist in looking for locks in every door, even one that's open? This is another of those questions related to Buñuel and his *Exterminating Angel.* Might not the fact of an open door's having a lock alter the status of its openness? And so on. In most instances, creating a culture necessarily means being acultural. For why, for the purposes of what he's creating, does a creative artist need to know what's being created by someone else? The creative artist can get by with fumbling about all over the place, since he knows very well that no amount of fumbling—no matter how far he might roam—can be limitless, or else it would spill over into something else. The role of the creator is to contain the imminent overspill in the actual nature of whatever the thing is, and to be deft enough to prevent it from really spilling over into something else. So what we're talking about here is the continual maintenance of the flow of that which is desired, which, for this very reason, unconditionally turns into what's being thought. Being thought in the sense of a tautology—something that can't be argued away. Being thought in the sense of the realization of an act of thinking, the context of which is that the flow of what's being thought is constantly recast as a flow of thought. This isn't philosophy, my friends, but the gradual process of deploying the creative urge, pneumatic drill in hand. The creative individual is more laborer than intellectual! *I say this: only people who are perverse in soul and body can perform great deeds!* So writes František Drtikol in one of his letters. And he goes on: *But it must be a perversion that is pure, beautiful, original, maverick, one that springs from man's own inner depths! It must not be something plagiarized, something picked up from elsewhere. . .* One thing that has a name, and another that is seeking a name. And then it transpires that the name doesn't go with what's designated, but with the act of designating. A leap into the identity of something that has legitimacy, because it has already been legitimized. A leap into the illusion of this critical fault, which—since, as a fault, it's entirely illusory—never ceases to seem critical. Like a thought that doesn't think about itself, but about what it isn't thinking about and about what it's detaching itself from by the act of disengaging from it. The mental process of the unfinished as aspiration. Ill-defined shouting. The claustrophobia of bothering oneself with it as with something of limited importance. Humor about the unfunny? But jokes have humor built in, don't they? I'm sitting on a bench in Prague's Little Quarter, shortly before midnight, musing as I settle down on what an antinomy actually is. And suddenly, emerging from a shock wave close by, a girl sits down near me. Something's burning on the next bench over. I urgently contemplate lighting a cigarette and finally do so. The tension between us was short-lived. I wanted to give her a chance, but she was impatient. She leapt noisily to her feet (all I registered was her delicate little nose and her glasses with their understated, thin rims) with the aim of executing a pirouette before my very eyes, spinning around on her heel to stamp out the cigarette butt of her desire in a gesture of scorn. But I didn't flinch. And a day later she appeared to me again in the form of a different woman. A no less noisy, intellectual type, with horn-rimmed spectacles and a flawless complexion. A girl who, after only a few days of our acquaintanceship, calls me on my cell phone to inform me that *I* need someone more refined. Laughter like a dog's barking, like the detonation of a response, a response to the unremitting impulse to respond that we call resignation. A response as a designation, as a brand. Response—the echo of a Narcissus to the tight-lipped companion of his dual desire. My attitude to women is monomagical. One always enters a situation unprepared, like the aftermath of sleep. Trying to make what's been survived vibrate with the tension of the chances of surviving. Finding the momentary window. Getting something wrong in an exam, as in a declarative sentence of contradiction. A man of flesh and blood develops a taste for humankind—the cannibal. Patterns of fertility, geysers of exorcism. The sun meandering through empty deposits of anxiety. A cohort of gratuitous resolutions meeting up behind enemy lines. The onto-topical fields of face-up hands of cards, onto-onomatopoeia. The tidy-minded progress of a tumor of the spirit toward being healed, away from its host body. And out of every pain a question mark pops up: Is this pain the right one? Blurring the invisible toward ever greater visibility. Escape manipulations, the coordinates of a cobweb cast into space. The insatiable cameras of untalented people who cough up bile wherever they go. Just opening their mouths like birds' beaks, from which the seeds of hate fall under the slightest pressure. A guy with three cell phones like three dicks, and opposite him a busty babe who's doing her damnedest to look serious, as if that were actually possible in her case. Two punks behind her react to a loud remark from the macho man, who gets up briefly to act out a screen test for the role of gunslinger without a gun, because right now he's enjoying himself. His girl has spent the last ten minutes in the toilet. One of the goons at the adjacent table relocates to her seat. The window-mirror through which I'm watching all this slowly mists over thanks to the unexpected way the evening is unfolding. For no obvious reason, they—one, another, the third—each wink at me in succession. As for me, I'm on form. I'm typing this nonsense into my head while ignoring the people I'm talking about. In one of the illustrations—those selfies of the naked L. that show her seeking and, here and there, spasmodically finding the true form of her physicality—there are two discolored patches on her neck, seen from the back, which in this photo looks even more androgynous than in reality. The bruise-like patches had obviously been painted in for effect, the photo not being in any sense documentary, and yet, for me, they have always been a memento, a visual meme that triggers a profusion of chain reactions of recrimination and self-recrimination. (What need is there to provoke demands in someone close to us, if it's a matter of getting them to change and they're already in the process of changing?) Wearing emotions on one's sleeve, as if inner feelings kept something concealed. An imposed denial of wanting, based on nothing, justified by nothing. A momentarily terrifying void is carved out both by a network-like structure and by the structure of breathing within it. Drink cans emptied of their contents rattle along a street of static sculptures newly filled with content of their own. Sights seen by tourist children and their braying cameras that rework what once was, including angels, into the form of other materials. The time shift between expectations and disappointments is shaky to the point of invisibility. This is about the extirpation of the sun and other solitudinarians of its ilk. It's about the tautology of every instant, as if every instant were perforce a tautology. "If I'd known she was so nuts, I definitely wouldn't have married her," Ben continues his story. And the sight of his interest in my work surpasses the consequences of my expectation. These reminiscences answer my need to remind him of me after all these years, since he no longer patrols my neighborhood, eavesdropping on me with an ear trumpet. What do Jan and Ben have in common? Nothing and a great deal. The former sees himself as a true liver of life, even to the extent of needing to lecture others on living. His faith in *re*production remains strong, despite the fact that he is still producing things. Ben hasn't started talking about reproduction yet, and even as an author he is almost unproductive. That notwithstanding, he exudes a sense of needing to change this state of affairs. Ben is secure against an appearance of solitariness through his marriage on paper, which from the outset obviously didn't suit him. The illusory security of this marital status, into which he plunged himself and his wife, is meant first and foremost to conceal something. Not even Ben believes in the irreversibility of his destiny—yet his actions, which seem to dog him, don't support this belief. One fact worth noting is that he's slightly the younger of the two, because even Jan, when he was Ben's age, perceived things similarly. Jan buzzed off out of a childless marriage, declaring that he had it in him to have other women as well. Ben probably thinks the same thing. Time was when both of them could be seen strolling around Prague in long black coats that accentuated their facade and the solidity of their standing even while they walked. One flirted with his artistic inclinations, the other theorized about them. Both had a positive attitude toward cats, but neither knew why. As long as their relationships lasted, both scrupulously observed their daily bachelor rituals. One is convinced that it's women who are supposed to tyrannize him, while the other is convinced of the reverse, a conviction that he fearlessly acts on in private. Their convictions are equally rock-solid, as especially evinced at the moment of ice-breaking. At that moment, they take notice, focus their senses, and with the finely chased shrieking of intellectuals they ruthlessly disavow themselves and the other. For a secret is generated by the removal of the secrecy behind something similar to it. The compunction to create resemblances? But anything that resembles is equidistant at all times from its original. This is about the shifting illusion that parades models before images of them capable of perceiving them. It's about reconfining the necessary into the form of that which, in the noise of contrast, has lost its own coloration. A Masada Quartet concert in a field somewhere, without a stage, the "givers" on the same level as the "receivers." But a certain natural distance between both groups of people, and with that the respect of the larger group for the smaller is sustained. Though admittedly, the few people making up the audience is suspiciously smaller than is usual at such concerts. Probably, no one's really been expecting the band to show up in such an out-of-the-way place, only a few yards, in fact, from our tower block on the Dúbravka project in Bratislava. The audience, hungry for an outlandish performance, is ready for almost anything. The band starts without any warm-up, diving straight in, which reminds me of the recording of their 1995 concerts in Taipei. At moments we can't distinguish between Zorn's saxophone imitating the shrieking of demons being exorcised and the howling of the wind across the meadow. Terézia is standing next to me, open-mouthed and wearing a childlike expression of disbelief. After half an hour's playing, there's an interval and the band is considerately hauled off to the resting-and-instrument-tuning zone. This is on the seventh floor of a tower block with a fairly spacious balcony. We—a small group of people—relish the sensation of being dazzled as we stride with the stellar band across the concrete of the projects. Terézia is screaming something, violently drawing attention to herself, as is her wont. Now we're inside the apartment. We let the band shake off the accumulated fatigue and prepare some modest refreshments. Still, no one comes out of the room we've set aside for resting. Suddenly, some strange sounds come from the room. Heartrending, then after a few dull blasts they gradually fall silent. Without warning, the musicians come running in confusion out of the room, as if needing help while at the same time resisting it. For a moment, the almost-bald trumpet player and the completely bald drummer look like doctors getting ready to perform an operation. They bind the momentarily limp Zorn—the band's leader—to a chair and lift him out onto the balcony. The bass player, wearing a baseball cap, wipes the soiled floor with a rag. Then all three of them bring some large object wrapped in polythene out of the resting room. On the balcony, someone wraps a white bandage around the mouth of the seated Zorn, who has begun to come round. They select someone, perform plenty of experiments on him, and only *ex post facto* describe him as the very object of the experiment. They misattribute any hidden meanings of his polysemous utterings to himself, though they treat them as unambiguous. They give him a hard time for years to come. What they, in an instant, stitch together with definitions he is forced to spend years unpicking by honest interpretation. Over time their definitions become so sclerotic that they grow rigid. His interpretations look as if they're made of butter, which they throw back in his face to have a good laugh at *his* babblings. They wind things up to the point where they find in all his babblings points with which to jab back at him from head to toe. In the blink of an eye, his defenses are instinctively engulfed by the need to rid the inner core of things of their inescapable outer shells. And this works, in return, against their inners, which it accordingly starts gnawing away. Two attributes of an observer: disdain and benevolence. Is it not those with the greatest stamina who abandon a sinking ship first? But then which ones are granted the ability to sense the bottom and draw specific lessons from the sensation? Is it possible that having a sense of the bottom is an option even in the event that we've been cast down there by force? If so, to what eventualities does this apply? The objectivity of obsessiveness? Let us do something, anything, and the moment it's done it ceases to be anything. There's here a kind of back-to-front conceptualism, a chance to find order in how one random event follows another. At the end there is always a concept, though in classical conceptualism the concept is at the beginning. So here is an exchange of one thing for another, which is undergoing constant interchange. We merely upscale the criteria, manipulating time in space by the number of pages written and suchlike. Any malfunction is a threshold event. The expected arrives unexpected. Building blocks of the mind, but how can the mind be a building? We would have to make allowance for its possible collapse at any moment. Pyromanticism. It never approaches maturity. And dreams are fended off like one volleyball after another (shots fired through a boat don't count). Possibility is inalienable. The character of man, the anthropomorphology of his very naturalness. The stuttering judgments of philosophers who, as far as the will is concerned, are lacking something. The antecedence of the age of the world's instruments over man. Workshops of ascendancy? Fanatics with a human face (wearing the devout countenance of praying mantises). How one actually thinks and, counterproductive to that, the actual thinking of others. Macrostics. When one illusion changes into another illusion, its essence remains unchanged. *Stay hungry! Stay foolish!*

And one may observe oneself communicating with a dead person who, in the rhotacizing tones of a girl's voice, is explaining to one how things always function piecemeal, whereby each piece contains within it the whole from which it has broken off despite itself, and, seeking a way out, points to this supplementarity with the defective *r* that automatically gets in the way of any, at first sight credible, chance of a future. There is nothing more manipulative than apprehensively fighting back against manipulation. Being the song of Job, insistent images fluttering about inside the heart in a ritual of rebirth. For all words uttered are like ants lining up in formation against you. Even errantry has paths to follow. One could speak of being freed of the compassion that necessarily follows from circumstances. In her case, this means that when they're dancing and she's twirling around them she's the only one who's not dancing. "But does someone have to go and jump off a bridge because of that?" the poet asks. "Yes," replies the dead girl's consciousness, which has been mysteriously silent in life. In her lifetime this consciousness had preferred hypotheses, which it immediately tested by destroying them. For example, it would always test the possibility of touching by touching, and so on. Even acts of coition seemed real, but how could they be real when they weren't? Liquid mercury introduced into a half-open mouth to compensate for bated breath is ill-advised. And yet, this was what she craved, after her consciousness had been chafed to possible nescience. For what other approach is there to a game in which what one's conscious of is attributed to the consciousness, to the latter's permanent disadvantage? Stories that begin at the end don't need beginnings that would convict them of making a point, that is, of committing a falsehood. A falsehood that loses its falsehood, being turned inside out by the truth, as if that were possible at first sight. But in any subculture there are other rules and privileges accorded to others that permit them to fire off viruses at everyone else, as if all that was at issue were the odd truth. As indeed is the case. Such truths have been hiding beneath the surface of inebriation and have usually been silent, because nobody would let them get a word in. Actually, attendees at these parties would subconsciously exchange them for falsehoods, as if they, whether truths or falsehoods, were immaterial. The point is that the seesawing certainties of these people prevented them from letting truth get a foothold. As if a prerequisite for the stability of a certain order were the prerequisite for stability even in an element that isn't stable. Watching bodiless souls being joined in a bouncy rhythm by soulless bodies. Giving over one's breath as an event that needs to be retold. Inner silence cannot capture it. Being silent outwardly means participating in building the temple. The monomorphism of being at every instant, each instant advancing under the impulse of obligation. Being as an analogue of breathing means denouncing breathing as something unnatural. The identity of the optional. Yes being entitled to Yes; likewise No. A consciousness that outstrips its own progression. First, one might believe and ask questions only afterward, or one might ask first and believe afterward. Flypaper keeps flies alive. In loving, what matters is not *who with*, but *how*. And the unity of opposites of pain. The zenithal moments of life in their conjunction with tight-lipped gobs. When not killing oneself, one's killing others, but those around are immune to it. Divers pasts of a diverse past (cast back from each point in the shade into a landscape of Platonic ideals). The anachronism of a vision that climaxes beneath a cloak of respite. Movement always complying with one and the same motion from the point of view of the goal. But a goal cannot be the arbiter of any point of view. My sorrow is organized by a sorrow that is organized. Little beetles, it says, have carried off the path to my person. Ever straying to the exact goal, as if straying had goals encoded into it. Visions of the instantaneous, not to be supported, not to be undermined. One can get sentimental even over a hangman, if you think about it. The monotony of any settled notion that, in its turn, turns any settled notion inside out. Torment is unending, but the form of its expression expresses something else. Fanatality. Raising doubts about the given, which is dubious only if the given is indubitable. The hands on a clock point to eternity at every moment of intransigence. But what kind of eternity is it when it persists only in an intake of breath and breathing actually harms it? Pain depicted through the variability of the meanings that, *ex post facto*, consign it to the cage of understanding. Having an understanding of somebody else is possible through both detachment and introspection. Both methods produce secondary static from the primary absence of understanding. A Yes won by obduracy is the product of having expected an unexpected No, which may spoil it. Containing oneself within a zone of inviolability, in order, if need be, to furtively pause and wonder. The furtive perception of a moment gulps in expectation of what it might perceive. So, its enjoyment is twofold, once in the anticipation and once in the inversion of it whereby any Yes of the present moment is but a vain rendering visible of something that effectively extends into the domain of what might be seen from the domain of what has been seen, which cannot be seen given that it is a direct component of our seeing. The bilateral uses blind alleys for the purpose of takeoff. We left the venue with a pleasant thrumming in our ears. “Your laughter is so infectious,” says D., radiant as an aspen. We toast life with a draught of corrosive. On the way to the toilet, one after the other, we watch those present and their shadows. A group of guys, Sex Pistols copycats, are just finishing their set. Encouraged, we’ve staggered off to another dive. Here we’re watching a girl with huge breasts and an uproarious top that does almost nothing to clothe them. The girl’s having a great time, downing one pint after another. D. says that there are no girls like that back home, alluding thereby to the invisible boundary between licentiousness born of a desire and licentiousness born of hysteria. Others would blame it on American girls’ innate tendency toward excess: they need to be outrageous in all circumstances. In another bar, D. unexpectedly asks me whether I’ve ever raised a hand against L. I no longer remember what my exact reply was, but I do remember that I hesitated. She nestled down in the leather seat and then stretched out like a flower about to burst from its bud. After letting her attention roam briefly but intensely around the sleazy interior, which is filling up with dozens of successful young men in suits, carrying briefcases, she says with seeming apathy: "Let's go." We've ended up on a motorcycle, where I hold her tenderly in my arms as if she were not one for rough play. Somebody had parked the motorcycle at the edge of a small square, which looked empty, but then it turned out that uniformed eavesdroppers can pop up from around every corner, if it comes to that. "We're going now," I say. I might have helped her break free from certain stereotypes, but she didn't need my help. She might have helped me break free from certain stereotypes, but I didn't need her help. Repetition is reminiscing ahead. Ineffectual dreams don't exist, so the unconscious is more effectual than consciousness. And since my pain doesn't follow from the findings of philosophy, the question is: In what respect can clarification of the cause of my pain be aided by the findings of philosophy? In being accountable for anything's enduring, since for what else can one be held accountable? This raises more questions: To what extent can the consciousness's accountability for something enduring be its consistent monitoring of it, and to what extent is the monitoring of what endures even conceivable and admissible? Is every story a manipulation? And so forth. A story is the span of a horizontal network needed for any vertical event to have something to grab hold of and evolve. The sheer intensity of the need for anticipation, which gradually mutates into a prophetic aptitude for precisely foreseeing what's already been called the future. The gradually identified dryness of a parched state and a cross turned upside down, uprooted into the firmament of the superego. Where a fall is a cry of victory, which, like an angel, comes crashing down with the result that, through the impact of what it has dragged down with it, it might blame some act of tearing asunder for that which has been catastrophically doomed *ab ovo* to be torn asunder. The dire straits of love. In the bright light of defiance. Light won through defiance? Fretful energy expended on trying to grab hold of and hold on to the aura of its lampposts. Years spent laboriously tempering one's capacity for feeling until the time comes when this capacity is transformed into the body's capacity for pain. But what kind of capacity is pain, when capacity means being able to act and achieve something? Is not even martyrdom, then, something that is by nature laughable, just as nature finds laughable any act of destruction or nihilism generated in the mind? On the basis of the natural need for words that are meant to be useful, one calls that semi-anonymous, self-promoting girl simply a prostitute. When faced with the incongruity of a rebus, we seek something invisibly our own. Being able to ask questions of that amiably chatty wee creature, even by means of a kiss, defined as mouth-to-mouth panting, as expressly offered in the girl's ad. "I do not require this service," I tell her decisively, but seeing her sincere, saddened eyes, my heart slowly mellows. I may not alter my decision, but I have a natural need to be at least as tender to her as she is to me. I feel the full effect of her embrace. It is maternal and soft, simultaneously affectionate and sensual. And without any pressure on any of the constraints of reality, including time. We prolonged our hour by almost an hour. Then having both come, we lie huddled together and keep quietly repeating something. It's eleven at night and I'm her last client of the day. I invite her for dinner and, much to my surprise, she accepts. I enjoy watching her panties sidewinding naturally over her smooth thighs to arrive safely, after a couple of wriggles and tugs, at the place where they belong. Finally, she tells me her name is Lu, which means "light." And now comes her story. When Lu got snagged in Ben's plans, the trap had been set long before. Lu had absolutely no objection to jumping right in. She appreciated how radical her decision was and therefore gave no thought to its further consequences. The Lost Childhood Club and other ghettos of ingenuity. The need we have for all the indispositions that impact on life is begging to be written about, but differently. "I'm used to phantoms now," says Ben, adding something about madness, which he says will never be within his grasp. The field of anxiety's inventiveness, craters of possibilities for anything tossed into the air like a geyser of playing cards. Ben nags at Lu for spending days on end doing nothing. She retorts that he had, if he hadn't forgotten, promised her work. He says he made no such promise. And she, that he did. And she burst into tears. He tried to soothe her, though he had an urge to slap her. She let herself be soothed, though she, too, had an urge to slap him. In the end, they made love and then got drunk. Such is the backdrop against which, for weeks and months, with only short breaks (for she would always leave for the east after a few weeks to see her parents), their cohabitation was played out. This setting was created by a chance observer. In calm tones he points out to someone what bothers him about me, but without bothering to add which bits he's only just invented. He says something about the exaggerated movements by which I cause turbulence in space and which he finds discordant. He used the addressee of this remark as a catalytic converter, because the remark was directed at me. Then he grinned, since seeing me as an object tallied with his job description. The worst writers are those who slowly evolve into the little top and bottom cogwheels that drive the mechanism of their own power, which needs constant organization because it's battery-driven. Its keyword is "cunt." If you're a man, you get up from the table slowly with a woman between your legs. "We think what we see; hence, we aren't seeing it," Ben maintains. "While others see what they're seeing because they don't think about what they see." He makes a great thing of Thomas Bernhard, whom he sets in a context of his own devising. However, in attempting to apply this truth to love, all he does is retreat from Bernhard back to the Kafka of one of the propositions in his *Letters to Milena*. In the event that the reader doesn't recognize the proposition, he can work it out for himself. I'm holding it like a dog—the thought crosses my mind in the metro—as I sense the heat of my hands slowly draining into a gently rounded metal bicycle frame. And, automatically following the thought through, I immediately add: a friend. D. and I are sitting in a small New York Bagel Buffet on Sixth Avenue, located just a few yards from Barnes & Noble's gigantic, multi-story bookstore. Together, we munch on slices of pizza, washing them down with hot half-and-half coffee. The flow of ideas that come springing into life is naturally synchronized to the gentle, but at that moment much-needed, soothing sound of the objects and people of life as it passes by. Baba Yaga's hut standing on a chicken leg. Somebody up there throws down a pair of eyeglasses. They are keys. They convey me up into a nest. I wonder, what was D. feeling as we stood crammed together in that corner like frozen flowers that aren't allowed to breathe? As the shrill shouting of melting lead had the two of us frostily shrieking with one and the same heart, which stepped up its output with every passing moment as a cycle of eternal, exhausting ecstasy flowed into its matching body. At first, she'd looked as if she didn't understand. "This is torture," she said. "Does he even know how to play that saxophone. . . ?" My reply to her, but kept to myself: "Positive negation is the negation of negation. There are various forms of such negation. From holding one's breath through the whole spectrum of colors that manifest themselves in monochrome, to the final gush spewing from the colorful spectrum of blood as it spills out from within and is, therefore, consistently authentic." So, no affinity based on nasal hair, then, D. ruminated as she tried to pinpoint just what it was about Hammano that appealed to her. He's got the complexion of a child, she continued to muse, as if unable to grasp how this child could be nearly fifty. He used to take me around with him like a little dog. Wait here, I'll be back in a mo. And he didn't come back till two hours later. As for my capacity for suffering, my endurance is considerable, D. says with an odd smirk. She describes to me the death of one of our friends I hadn't seen for years. One after another his organs had failed, finally he'd gone blind and from then on he never went out. He was a mathematical genius whose greatest mistake was not to have left Slovakia after the November revolution. Today he'd have a post at Oxford, a steady income, and he'd probably have resisted the snares of alcoholism. What horrified me most was the dry tone in which she was telling me all this, as if she wasn't even talking about a human being, but about a mass of inert matter condemned to the decomposition that she was idly contemplating with the eyes of a voyeur. What does she actually see in Hammano, I ponder, summoning up a mental image of that life-sated artist, who once plunged an embryonic Christ on the Cross into a bottle of weird moonshine and called the work, with fitting effrontery, *Original Sin*? But just go try and identify with your own name and what it evokes by way of an icon. "I am not I," says Hammano, because he is Hammano and he's right, even though he's wrong. And that's why. In any tautology lurks a concentrated empathy for tautologically opening up that which has been opened. She had the jitters before entering the venue. She dithered outside the entrance, and if I hadn't gone out for a smoke, she might have sneaked away altogether. I catch her by the shoulder: "Come on, for goodness' sake!" She says she's going to buy a ticket first, and so she does. We sense an affinity with the space that's slowly closing in. We're standing together, suitably apart from each other. The squall of tones from the first piece of the concert casts us both into apathetic expectation of the inevitability to come. When years emanate from days. These are Mondays, these Sundays, and so on. This is a shadow of light, and this is the sun. Night is also a sun. His need to communicate has never been desperate, but even so, it has agreed to elicit disagreeing reactions from the critics. They would pick on various imperfections in his work, which was never meant to be perfect, because it needed to breathe. "I'm so relaxed," says D. in the bath, "that I could happily drown myself." And the reality of what he's seeing automatically adjusts to being seen. If on occasion liquid honey overflows, it turns into. . . The need to open one's eyes, which must perforce see something, surely. Something that, in order to be seen, even if it's not far from itself, is nonetheless brought closer to itself by means of revelation. Opening one's eyes and thus being able to see something that might strike the need to dream as invisible. The moments before her execution could not be captured for the simple reason that the entire execution happened so fast that it really couldn't be recaptured. What took place in the sequel was merely an amplification of the first step leading up to it (the execution) by its ever more drawn out deceleration in the hallucinogenic haze of a decision that at the time still might not even have been realized. He rummaged around in her with his eyes, his sordid fingers, and she, head thrown back, breathed in and out. Her lightly trembling lips slightly parted the surface of her otherwise tightly clamped mouth. Depurgation? The plane to New York is leaving shortly. A shrink-wrapped laptop, a Brompton bicycle, and a bag of clothes are ready. Just before takeoff I dab a little snake of fresh toothpaste on one hand of several of my fellow travelers, including the passport and boarding pass guys. Let us remind ourselves of the subjects of conversations conducted in languages with a limited range of words, cut down to rhetorical figures and configurations. Colleagues from New York's universities eager for diplomas in flashy frames never stop rubbing in how much of a good-for-nothing I am, as if being good for something were a role for everybody. As if I, too, should be one of the cogs in the mechanism by which other cogs function. A poet is dead before he's even born—especially in a small country. And I wonder: To what extent is distrust of Yes more intrinsic to *discovering* than to *seeking*, and wherein resides the proto-Yes of the question to which our mind defensively answers No? And how does the infinity between opposing constraints differ from the infinity between two infinities? I may never have read the Bible, but whenever I open it at a random page, it speaks to me in sentences that I've lived, uttered, and, as truths, interiorized. So where's the need to know history? Isn't it enough to be a part of it? For many years there have been three men in particular who have inspired me and helped refine my faculty (and aptitude) for a critical awareness of reality. Thomas Bernhard, the master of tautology; Georges Bataille, the master of metaphysical excess; and the master of hysterico-ontological, postmodern manipulation, John Zorn. And if I'm to go on, then I'll mention how these three creative spirits relate to the subject of the boundary between the possibility of opting for evil, including the option to become its victim, and the evil that is part and parcel of reality, hence there can be absolutely no talk of opting for it. (But is not the exhaustion that arises from exercising a right merely the obverse of the exhaustion of meeting an obligation?) At the moment of our anguished connecting-up to heaven, the very closeness of the connection becomes manifest. Initially with no face, invisibly as it were, but later, prefiguring the face's features means to have been exploring them with our various senses, which, in a process of coordinated structuring, complement each other and advance into an ever more complex unit of territory. But what sort of unit is it, and what sort of territory, which by demarcating the whole gives it its integrity? And what is the everything that is exceptionally created for the needs of its creator? How can these needs be demarcated, and why should that even be possible? Is any question that demarcates a demarcation *eo ipso* always blasphemous? And even if it were, shall we dismiss it? Agnomia.

Berlin, New York, Prague
January 2007–February 2008

SELECTED DALKEY ARCHIVE TITLES

MICHAL AJVAZ, *The Golden Age. The Other City.*
PIERRE ALBERT-BIROT, *Grabinoulor.*
YUZ ALESHKOVSKY, *Kangaroo.*
FELIPE ALFAU, *Chromos. Locos.*
JOE AMATO, *Samuel Taylor's Last Night.*
IVAN ÂNGELO, *The Celebration. The Tower of Glass.*
ANTÓNIO LOBO ANTUNES, *Knowledge of Hell. The Splendor of Portugal.*
ALAIN ARIAS-MISSON, *Theatre of Incest.*
JOHN ASHBERY & JAMES SCHUYLER, *A Nest of Ninnies.*
ROBERT ASHLEY, *Perfect Lives.*
GABRIELA AVIGUR-ROTEM, *Heatwave and Crazy Birds.*
DJUNA BARNES, *Ladies Almanack. Ryder.*
JOHN BARTH, *Letters. Sabbatical.*
DONALD BARTHELME, *The King. Paradise.*
SVETISLAV BASARA, *Chinese Letter.*
MIQUEL BAUÇÀ, *The Siege in the Room.*
RENÉ BELLETTO, *Dying.*
MAREK BIENCZYK, *Transparency.*
ANDREI BITOV, *Pushkin House.*
ANDREJ BLATNIK, *You Do Understand. Law of Desire.*
LOUIS PAUL BOON, *Chapel Road. My Little War. Summer in Termuren.*
ROGER BOYLAN, *Killoyle.*
IGNÁCIO DE LOYOLA BRANDÃO, *Anonymous Celebrity. Zero.*
BONNIE BREMSER, *Troia: Mexican Memoirs.*
CHRISTINE BROOKE-ROSE, *Amalgamemnon.*
BRIGID BROPHY, *In Transit. The Prancing Novelist.*
GERALD L. BRUNS, *Modern Poetry and the Idea of Language.*
GABRIELLE BURTON, *Heartbreak Hotel.*
MICHEL BUTOR, *Degrees. Mobile.*
G. CABRERA INFANTE, *Infante's Inferno. Three Trapped Tigers.*
JULIETA CAMPOS, *The Fear of Losing Eurydice.*
ANNE CARSON, *Eros the Bittersweet.*
ORLY CASTEL-BLOOM, *Dolly City.*
LOUIS-FERDINAND CÉLINE, *North. Conversations with Professor Y. London Bridge.*
MARIE CHAIX, *The Laurels of Lake Constance.*
HUGO CHARTERIS, *The Tide Is Right.*
ERIC CHEVILLARD, *Demolishing Nisard. The Author and Me.*
MARC CHOLODENKO, *Mordechai Schamz.*
JOSHUA COHEN, *Witz.*
EMILY HOLMES COLEMAN, *The Shutter of Snow.*
ERIC CHEVILLARD, *The Author and Me.*
ROBERT COOVER, *A Night at the Movies.*
STANLEY CRAWFORD, *Log of the S.S. The Mrs Unguentine. Some Instructions to My Wife.*
RENÉ CREVEL, *Putting My Foot in It.*
RALPH CUSACK, *Cadenza.*
NICHOLAS DELBANCO, *Sherbrookes. The Count of Concord.*

FOR A FULL LIST OF PUBLICATIONS, VISIT: www.dalkeyarchive.com

SELECTED DALKEY ARCHIVE TITLES

NIGEL DENNIS, *Cards of Identity.*

PETER DIMOCK, *A Short Rhetoric for Leaving the Family.*

ARIEL DORFMAN, *Konfidenz.*

COLEMAN DOWELL, *Island People.*
Too Much Flesh and Jabez.

ARKADII DRAGOMOSHCHENKO, *Dust.*

RIKKI DUCORNET, *Phosphor in Dreamland.*
The Complete Butcher's Tales.

RIKKI DUCORNET (cont.), *The Jade Cabinet.*
The Fountains of Neptune.

WILLIAM EASTLAKE, *The Bamboo Bed.*
Castle Keep.
Lyric of the Circle Heart.

JEAN ECHENOZ, *Chopin's Move.*

STANLEY ELKIN, *A Bad Man.*
Criers and Kibitzers, Kibitzers and Criers.
The Dick Gibson Show.
The Franchiser.
The Living End.
Mrs. Ted Bliss.

FRANÇOIS EMMANUEL, *Invitation to a Voyage.*

PAUL EMOND, *The Dance of a Sham.*

SALVADOR ESPRIU, *Ariadne in the Grotesque Labyrinth.*

LESLIE A. FIEDLER, *Love and Death in the American Novel.*

JUAN FILLOY, *Op Oloop.*

ANDY FITCH, *Pop Poetics.*

GUSTAVE FLAUBERT, *Bouvard and Pécuchet.*

KASS FLEISHER, *Talking out of School.*

JON FOSSE, *Aliss at the Fire.*
Melancholy.

FORD MADOX FORD, *The March of Literature.*

MAX FRISCH, *I'm Not Stiller.*
Man in the Holocene.

CARLOS FUENTES, *Christopher Unborn.*
Distant Relations.
Terra Nostra.
Where the Air Is Clear.

TAKEHIKO FUKUNAGA, *Flowers of Grass.*

WILLIAM GADDIS, JR., *The Recognitions.*

JANICE GALLOWAY, *Foreign Parts.*
The Trick Is to Keep Breathing.

WILLIAM H. GASS, *Life Sentences.*
The Tunnel.
The World Within the Word.
Willie Masters' Lonesome Wife.

GÉRARD GAVARRY, *Hoppla! 1 2 3.*

ETIENNE GILSON, *The Arts of the Beautiful.*
Forms and Substances in the Arts.

C. S. GISCOMBE, *Giscome Road.*
Here.

DOUGLAS GLOVER, *Bad News of the Heart.*

WITOLD GOMBROWICZ, *A Kind of Testament.*

PAULO EMÍLIO SALES GOMES, *P's Three Women.*

GEORGI GOSPODINOV, *Natural Novel.*

JUAN GOYTISOLO, *Count Julian.*
Juan the Landless.
Makbara.
Marks of Identity.

HENRY GREEN, *Blindness.*
Concluding.
Doting.
Nothing.

JACK GREEN, *Fire the Bastards!*

JIŘÍ GRUŠA, *The Questionnaire.*

MELA HARTWIG, *Am I a Redundant Human Being?*

JOHN HAWKES, *The Passion Artist.*
Whistlejacket.

ELIZABETH HEIGHWAY, ED., *Contemporary Georgian Fiction.*

AIDAN HIGGINS, *Balcony of Europe.*
Blind Man's Bluff.
Bornholm Night-Ferry.
Langrishe, Go Down.
Scenes from a Receding Past.
KEIZO HINO, *Isle of Dreams.*
KAZUSHI HOSAKA, *Plainsong.*
ALDOUS HUXLEY, *Antic Hay.*
Point Counter Point.
Those Barren Leaves.
Time Must Have a Stop.
NAOYUKI II, *The Shadow of a Blue Cat.*
DRAGO JANČAR, *The Tree with No Name.*
MIKHEIL JAVAKHISHVILI, *Kvachi.*
GERT JONKE, *The Distant Sound.*
Homage to Czerny.
The System of Vienna.
JACQUES JOUET, *Mountain R.*
Savage.
Upstaged.
MIEKO KANAI, *The Word Book.*
YORAM KANIUK, *Life on Sandpaper.*
ZURAB KARUMIDZE, *Dagny.*
JOHN KELLY, *From Out of the City.*
HUGH KENNER, *Flaubert, Joyce and Beckett: The Stoic Comedians.*
Joyce's Voices.
DANILO KIŠ, *The Attic.*
The Lute and the Scars.
Psalm 44.
A Tomb for Boris Davidovich.
ANITA KONKKA, *A Fool's Paradise.*
GEORGE KONRÁD, *The City Builder.*
TADEUSZ KONWICKI, *A Minor Apocalypse.*
The Polish Complex.
ANNA KORDZAIA-SAMADASHVILI, *Me, Margarita.*
MENIS KOUMANDAREAS, *Koula.*
ELAINE KRAF, *The Princess of 72nd Street.*
JIM KRUSOE, *Iceland.*
AYSE KULIN, *Farewell: A Mansion in Occupied Istanbul.*
EMILIO LASCANO TEGUI, *On Elegance While Sleeping.*
ERIC LAURRENT, *Do Not Touch.*
VIOLETTE LEDUC, *La Bâtarde.*
EDOUARD LEVÉ, *Autoportrait.*
Newspaper.
Suicide.
Works.
MARIO LEVI, *Istanbul Was a Fairy Tale.*
DEBORAH LEVY, *Billy and Girl.*
JOSÉ LEZAMA LIMA, *Paradiso.*
ROSA LIKSOM, *Dark Paradise.*
OSMAN LINS, *Avalovara.*
The Queen of the Prisons of Greece.
FLORIAN LIPUŠ, *The Errors of Young Tjaž.*
GORDON LISH, *Peru.*
ALF MACLOCHLAINN, *Out of Focus.*
Past Habitual.
The Corpus in the Library.
RON LOEWINSOHN, *Magnetic Field(s).*
YURI LOTMAN, *Non-Memoirs.*
D. KEITH MANO, *Take Five.*
MINA LOY, *Stories and Essays of Mina Loy.*
MICHELINE AHARONIAN MARCOM,
A Brief History of Yes.
The Mirror in the Well.
BEN MARCUS, *The Age of Wire and String.*
WALLACE MARKFIELD, *Teitlebaum's Window.*
DAVID MARKSON, *Reader's Block.*
Wittgenstein's Mistress.
CAROLE MASO, *AVA.*
HISAKI MATSUURA, *Triangle.*
LADISLAV MATEJKA &

SELECTED DALKEY ARCHIVE TITLES

KRYSTYNA POMORSKA, EDS., *Readings in Russian Poetics: Formalist & Structuralist Views.*

HARRY MATHEWS, *Cigarettes.*
The Conversions.
The Human Country.
The Journalist.
My Life in CIA.
Singular Pleasures.
The Sinking of the Odradek.
Stadium.
Tlooth.

HISAKI MATSUURA, *Triangle.*

DONAL MCLAUGHLIN, *beheading the virgin mary, and other stories.*

JOSEPH MCELROY, *Night Soul and Other Stories.*

ABDELWAHAB MEDDEB, *Talismano.*

GERHARD MEIER, *Isle of the Dead.*

HERMAN MELVILLE, *The Confidence-Man.*

AMANDA MICHALOPOULOU, *I'd Like.*

STEVEN MILLHAUSER, *The Barnum Museum.*
In the Penny Arcade.

RALPH J. MILLS, JR., *Essays on Poetry.*

MOMUS, *The Book of Jokes.*

CHRISTINE MONTALBETTI, *The Origin of Man.*
Western.

NICHOLAS MOSLEY, *Accident.*
Assassins.
Catastrophe Practice.
A Garden of Trees.
Hopeful Monsters.
Imago Bird.
Inventing God.
Look at the Dark.
Metamorphosis.
Natalie Natalia.
Serpent.

WARREN MOTTE, *Fables of the Novel: French Fiction since 1990.*
Fiction Now: The French Novel in the 21st Century.
Mirror Gazing.
Oulipo: A Primer of Potential Literature.

GERALD MURNANE, *Barley Patch.*
Inland.

YVES NAVARRE, *Our Share of Time.*
Sweet Tooth.

DOROTHY NELSON, *In Night's City.*
Tar and Feathers.

ESHKOL NEVO, *Homesick.*

WILFRIDO D. NOLLEDO, *But for the Lovers.*

BORIS A. NOVAK, *The Master of Insomnia.*

FLANN O'BRIEN, *At Swim-Two-Birds.*
The Best of Myles.
The Dalkey Archive.
The Hard Life.
The Poor Mouth.
The Third Policeman.

CLAUDE OLLIER, *The Mise-en-Scène.*
Wert and the Life Without End.

PATRIK OUŘEDNÍK, *Europeana.*
The Opportune Moment, 1855.

BORIS PAHOR, *Necropolis.*

FERNANDO DEL PASO, *News from the Empire.*
Palinuro of Mexico.

ROBERT PINGET, *The Inquisitory.*
Mahu or The Material.
Trio.

MANUEL PUIG, *Betrayed by Rita Hayworth.*
The Buenos Aires Affair.
Heartbreak Tango.

RAYMOND QUENEAU, *The Last Days.*
Odile.
Pierrot Mon Ami.
Saint Glinglin.

ANN QUIN, *Berg.*
Passages.
Three.
Tripticks.

ISHMAEL REED, *The Free-Lance*

Pallbearers.
The Last Days of Louisiana Red.
Ishmael Reed: The Plays.
Juice!
The Terrible Threes.
The Terrible Twos.
Yellow Back Radio Broke-Down.

JASIA REICHARDT, *15 Journeys Warsaw to London.*

JOÃO UBALDO RIBEIRO, *House of the Fortunate Buddhas.*

JEAN RICARDOU, *Place Names.*

RAINER MARIA RILKE, *The Notebooks of Malte Laurids Brigge.*

JULIÁN RÍOS, *The House of Ulysses.*
Larva: A Midsummer Night's Babel.
Poundemonium.

ALAIN ROBBE-GRILLET, *Project for a Revolution in New York.*
A Sentimental Novel.

AUGUSTO ROA BASTOS, *I the Supreme.*

DANIËL ROBBERECHTS, *Arriving in Avignon.*

JEAN ROLIN, *The Explosion of the Radiator Hose.*

OLIVIER ROLIN, *Hotel Crystal.*

ALIX CLEO ROUBAUD, *Alix's Journal.*

JACQUES ROUBAUD, *The Form of a City Changes Faster, Alas, Than the Human Heart.*
The Great Fire of London.
Hortense in Exile.
Hortense Is Abducted.
Mathematics: The Plurality of Worlds of Lewis.
Some Thing Black.

RAYMOND ROUSSEL, *Impressions of Africa.*

VEDRANA RUDAN, *Night.*

PABLO M. RUIZ, *Four Cold Chapters on the Possibility of Literature.*

GERMAN SADULAEV, *The Maya Pill.*

TOMAŽ ŠALAMUN, *Soy Realidad.*

LYDIE SALVAYRE, *The Company of Ghosts.*
The Lecture.
The Power of Flies.

LUIS RAFAEL SÁNCHEZ, *Macho Camacho's Beat.*

SEVERO SARDUY, *Cobra & Maitreya.*

NATHALIE SARRAUTE, *Do You Hear Them?*
Martereau.
The Planetarium.

STIG SÆTERBAKKEN, *Siamese.*
Self-Control.
Through the Night.

ARNO SCHMIDT, *Collected Novellas.*
Collected Stories.
Nobodaddy's Children.
Two Novels.

ASAF SCHURR, *Motti.*

GAIL SCOTT, *My Paris.*

DAMION SEARLS, *What We Were Doing and Where We Were Going.*

JUNE AKERS SEESE, *Is This What Other Women Feel Too?*

BERNARD SHARE, *Inish.*
Transit.

VIKTOR SHKLOVSKY, *Bowstring.*
Literature and Cinematography.
Theory of Prose.
Third Factory.
Zoo, or Letters Not about Love.

PIERRE SINIAC, *The Collaborators.*

KJERSTI A. SKOMSVOLD, *The Faster I Walk, the Smaller I Am.*

JOSEF ŠKVORECKÝ, *The Engineer of Human Souls.*

GILBERT SORRENTINO, *Aberration of Starlight.*
Blue Pastoral.
Crystal Vision.
Imaginative Qualities of Actual Things.
Mulligan Stew. Red the Fiend.
Steelwork.
Under the Shadow.

SELECTED DALKEY ARCHIVE TITLES

MARKO SOSIČ, *Ballerina, Ballerina.*
ANDRZEJ STASIUK, *Dukla.*
Fado.
GERTRUDE STEIN, *The Making of Americans.*
A Novel of Thank You.
LARS SVENDSEN, *A Philosophy of Evil.*
PIOTR SZEWC, *Annihilation.*
GONÇALO M. TAVARES, *A Man: Klaus Klump.*
Jerusalem.
Learning to Pray in the Age of Technique.
LUCIAN DAN TEODOROVICI, *Our Circus Presents . . .*
NIKANOR TERATOLOGEN, *Assisted Living.*
STEFAN THEMERSON, *Hobson's Island.*
The Mystery of the Sardine.
Tom Harris.
TAEKO TOMIOKA, *Building Waves.*
JOHN TOOMEY, *Sleepwalker.*
DUMITRU TSEPENEAG, *Hotel Europa.*
The Necessary Marriage.
Pigeon Post.
Vain Art of the Fugue.
ESTHER TUSQUETS, *Stranded.*
DUBRAVKA UGRESIC, *Lend Me Your Character.*
Thank You for Not Reading.
TOR ULVEN, *Replacement.*
MATI UNT, *Brecht at Night.*
Diary of a Blood Donor.
Things in the Night.
ÁLVARO URIBE & OLIVIA SEARS, EDS.,
Best of Contemporary Mexican Fiction.
ELOY URROZ, *Friction.*
The Obstacles.
LUISA VALENZUELA, *Dark Desires and the Others.*
He Who Searches.
PAUL VERHAEGHEN, *Omega Minor.*
BORIS VIAN, *Heartsnatcher.*
LLORENÇ VILLALONGA, *The Dolls' Room.*
TOOMAS VINT, *An Unending Landscape.*
ORNELA VORPSI, *The Country Where No One Ever Dies.*
AUSTRYN WAINHOUSE, *Hedyphagetica.*
CURTIS WHITE, *America's Magic Mountain.*
The Idea of Home.
Memories of My Father Watching TV.
Requiem.
DIANE WILLIAMS,
Excitability: Selected Stories.
Romancer Erector.
DOUGLAS WOOLF, *Wall to Wall.*
Ya! & John-Juan.
JAY WRIGHT, *Polynomials and Pollen.*
The Presentable Art of Reading Absence.
PHILIP WYLIE, *Generation of Vipers.*
MARGUERITE YOUNG, *Angel in the Forest.*
Miss MacIntosh, My Darling.
REYOUNG, *Unbabbling.*
VLADO ŽABOT, *The Succubus.*
ZORAN ŽIVKOVIĆ , *Hidden Camera.*
LOUIS ZUKOFSKY, *Collected Fiction.*
VITOMIL ZUPAN, *Minuet for Guitar.*
SCOTT ZWIREN, *God Head.*

AND MORE . . .

FOR A FULL LIST OF PUBLICATIONS, VISIT: www.dalkeyarchive.com

www.ingramcontent.com/pod-product-compliance
Lightning Source LLC
Chambersburg PA
CBHW030417120726
47904CB00007B/2311
* 9 7 8 1 6 2 8 9 7 2 7 9 5 *